Noah's Park

SHOWDOWN AT SCREECH'S HOLLOW

Written by Richard Hays
Illustrated by Chris Sharp

Faith Kids

Faith Kids®

is an imprint of Cook Communications Ministries,
Colorado Springs, Colorado 80918
Cook Communications, Paris, Ontario
Kingsway Communications, Eastbourne, England

SHOWDOWN AT SCREECH'S HOLLOW
©2001 by The Illustrated Word, Inc.

First printing, 2001
Printed in Canada
05 04 03 02 01   5 4 3 2 1

Digital art and design: Gary Currant
Executive Producer: Kenneth R. Wilcox

Showdown At Screech's Hollow

Life Issue: My children need to learn to appreciate others.
Spiritual Building Block: Respect
Learning Styles: Help your children to gain respect for others in the following ways:

Sight: When a child in your home ends up with hurt feelings, ask the other children to look at her face. Ask them if they remember a time they felt that way. Explain that hurt feelings can be avoided if we would all care for each other as much as we care for ourselves. Then be sure to ask the sad child if you all could give her a hug and say sorry.

Sound: Ask your children to choose a secret hour to test your family's "respecting skills." Tell them to tally up all the times someone spoke unkind words or acted disrespectful to another family member during that hour. When they give the report at the end of the hour, make a family goal to do better during the next pop quiz.

Touch: Cuddle with your children on the couch while you read Showdown and other books to your kids. Let them stay with you until they choose to wander away. When you model a respectful attitude by honoring their needs for affection and attention, they will be more willing to respect others.

One hot afternoon in Noah's Park, Screech the monkey huffed and puffed as he rolled a boulder into a ditch.

"This is hard work," he grumbled to himself. After three days of back-breaking work, the path from the beach to his tree was finally finished.

Screech scampered up into the tree and picked
a spot where three huge limbs joined together.
It was perfect for what he had in mind. He rubbed
the smooth bark. He loved how it felt. In fact,
Screech loved everything about the amazing tree.
He was sure that a tree as wonderful as this
could only be a gift from God. Screech
was also sure that it had been no
accident that he and not his best
friend Shadow the raccoon had
found the tree while they were
playing hide and seek.

Screech paused. For a moment he felt bad for Shadow. The two lived together in a tree by the waterfall, and Shadow might not like what Screech was doing.

Shadow would probably be happy for him. He shrugged.

Screech skipped out of the tree and up to the beach where Honk the camel had his workshop. There were partially completed projects sitting everywhere.

"What's that, Honk?" asked Screech.

"It's a thing to clean the dirt off the beach. I'm going to call it Honk's Thing to Clean the Dirt Off the Beach," said Honk proudly.

"Catchy," chirped Screech, rolling his eyes.

"I need to borrow some tools, Honk," Screech said. "I want to build something."

"Sure, Screech. Would you like to help, too?" Honk asked. "I'm really getting the hang of this inventing thing."

Screech looked around at the odd collection of unfinished inventions. None of them looked as if they were ever going to do anything at all.

"No," he said slowly, "I think I'll just take the tools."

Screech began his project in the big tree the next day. First, he used small tree saplings to build a floor. It took him all day. The next day he gathered large palm leaves and tied them together for walls. He carefully cut out windows in each of the four walls.

On the third and last day, Screech built a roof. He rubbed mud into the roof so the leaves would not blow away. As the sun set, Screech sat down on the floor and admired his work. His new home was complete.

As Screech settled into his treehouse, he decided his new home was missing just one thing: a name. Smiling, he decided he would call it Screech's Hollow.

Screech dropped to the
ground and looked back at the tree.
He couldn't take his eyes off his new home.

"Is that our new fort?" asked Shadow. "It looks
great! Why didn't you let me help you?"

Startled, Screech jumped straight up into the
air. Then he whirled around and saw Shadow
looking at the treehouse. "Oh, Shadow, uh, hi.
Our new fort? Well, no, I ... I've been wanting
a new place to live, and, well, when I saw
this tree, I knew it was the place for
me. This is my new home." Screech
smiled, weakly waving his hands
and looking at his feet.

"I was going to tell
you later."

"You're going to live in this tree ... without me?" Shadow said in disbelief. "How can you do that to your best friend? Why didn't you tell me? I thought you had more respect for me. Boy, Screech, you've pulled some tricks in your time, but this is the worst one of all. This isn't fair. I'm going to get even. You just better watch out!" Shadow spun around and stomped away.

"Shadow? Shadow? Wait," Screech called softly, but Shadow did not turn around. He was gone, and Screech felt horrible. He was also very worried.

That night Screech stayed in his new home for the first time. He felt sad. He had thought he would have a party to celebrate his new home, but Ponder the frog had traveled up the river for some new seeds, and Shadow was really the only other animal in Noah's Park that could fit in the treehouse. The only other except, of course, for ...

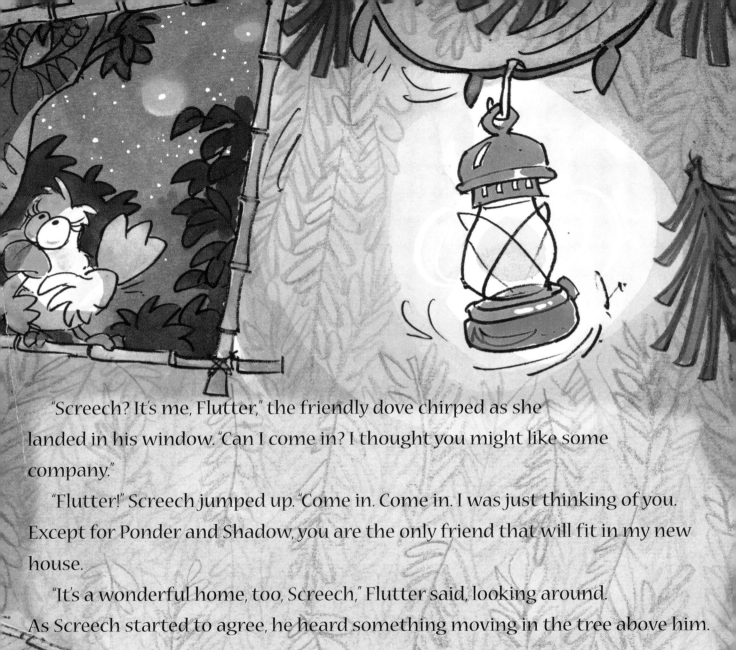

"Screech? It's me, Flutter," the friendly dove chirped as she
landed in his window. "Can I come in? I thought you might like some
company."

"Flutter!" Screech jumped up. "Come in. Come in. I was just thinking of you.
Except for Ponder and Shadow, you are the only friend that will fit in my new
house.

"It's a wonderful home, too, Screech," Flutter said, looking around.
As Screech started to agree, he heard something moving in the tree above him.

He glanced up just in time to see his roof come crashing down under a hailstorm of coconuts.

"Arggh!" screamed Screech as he and Flutter jumped out of the window. Screech hit the ground rolling. He looked up and saw Shadow swinging from a vine, knocking down part of a wall with his feet with each swing.

"No, Shadow! Don't do it!" screeched Screech. "You're wrecking my house."

But Shadow continued until there was no roof or walls left standing.

In just a few minutes, Shadow had destroyed Screech's home!

The next day Honk, Shadow, Ivory the elephant, and Dreamer the rhinoceros were resting on the beach. Ponder had returned and was telling them about his adventures on the river.

"It was amazing," Ponder was saying, "how many different kinds of fruit there were growing along the river. I counted more than twenty kinds of berries alone."

"That makes my mouth water!" exclaimed Ivory.
"I love berries."

Suddenly, Screech marched into the group and threw
a banana peel down on the ground in front of Shadow.
"Shadow," said Screech, "I'm calling you out. You said that I did
not show you respect, but I didn't wreck your home like you wrecked mine.
We're going to have a showdown right now at Screech's Hollow ... where I used
to have a home!"

Ponder hopped quickly as he tried to keep up with Shadow, who was marching angrily after Screech.

"I really think this a bad idea," the wise frog said. "You or Screech might get hurt! And what will God think of two best friends fighting? Neither one of you is showing any respect for the other."

Shadow just kept walking. At Screech's Hollow, all the other animals were waiting. Screech stood by a large pile of coconuts. Another pile waited for Shadow.

"When I count to three," said Screech, "start throwing, Shadow. Whoever is still standing at the end gets the tree and Screech's Hollow."

Suddenly, the air in Screech's Hollow became very still. Even the sun seemed warmer. Dreamer looked at Ponder as if to ask, "Are we really going to let this happen?"

Ponder shrugged his shoulders as if to say, "What can we do?"

Screech started counting.

"One ... two ... THREE!"

Screech and Shadow each grabbed a coconut and threw. Screech's coconut bounced off a tree and hit Ponder, Dreamer, and Honk in their heads.

Shadow's coconut boomeranged
off another tree and knocked down
Ivory, Howler, and Stretch.

Screech and Shadow quickly reached for another coconut and started to throw again. Then, just as quickly, both of them dropped their coconuts and began to cry.

"I can't do it, Shadow," wept Screech. "Even though you destroyed my home, I guess I still do have respect for you. You can have the tree and make your own home."

"I can't do it, either, Screech," blubbered Shadow. "I respect you, too. You're still my best friend. I'm really sorry I wrecked your house. I'm going to help you rebuild so you have your space."

Screech looked at Shadow and smiled. "Let's rebuild it and live here together. I have an idea so we can both have plenty of space and plenty of respect for each other."

Screech and Shadow laughed and hugged. The other animals, while still dazed and certainly surprised at this turn of events, applauded.

"That was a close one, God." Ponder chuckled as he floated on Polka Dot Pond that evening. Screech and Shadow were still working on their new house. It was going to be a double-decker.

"I just need to have more faith in you and in my friends. They learn to do the right thing by having these experiences, and, even though sometimes the lessons are painful," he said, rubbing his sore head, "I need to respect that."

The End

DREAMER HAS A NIGHTMARE

Dreamer the rhinoceros loves to dream, until one day he has his first nightmare. How will Dreamer handle this frightening experience? Discover the answer in the Noah's Park adventure, *Dreamer Has a Nightmare*.

STRETCH'S TREASURE HUNT

Stretch the giraffe grew up watching her parents search for the Treasure of Nosy Rock. Imagine what happens when she finds out that the treasure might be buried in Noah's Park. Watch the fur fly as Stretch and her friends look for treasure in *Stretch's Treasure Hunt*.

CAMELS DON'T FLY

Honk the camel finds a statue of a camel with wings. Now, he is convinced that he can fly, too. Will Honk be the first camel to fly? Find out in the Noah's Park adventure, *Camels Don't Fly*.

HONK'S BIG ADVENTURE

On the first day of spring, all the animals of Noah's Park are playing in the mud, water, and leaves. This good clean fun creates a lot of dirty animals. When Honk the camel sees the mess, he decides to leave Noah's Park and find a clean place to live. Will Honk find what he searches for? Find out in the hilarious Noah's Park story, *Honk's Big Adventure*.

PONDER MEETS THE POLKA DOTS

Ponder the frog is growing lily pads in the Noah's Park pond. When something starts eating the lily pads, the normally calm frog decides to get even. Will Ponder save his lily pads? Find out in the colorful Noah's Park adventure, *Ponder Meets the Polka Dots*.